Prai: **THE RETRIEVAL** ....

D1555462

One of the top ten greatest science fiction detectives of all time.

—io9

The SF thriller is alive and well, and today's leading practitioner is Kristine Kathryn Rusch.

—Analog

[Miles Flint is] one of 14 great sci-fi and fantasy detectives who out-Sherlock'd Holmes. [Flint] is a candidate for the title of greatest fictional detective of all time.

—Blastr

If there's any such thing as a sci-fi *CSI*, the Retrieval Artist novels set the tone.

—The Edge Boston

What links [Miles Flint] to his most memorable literary ancestors is his hard-won ability to perceive the complex nature of morality and live with the burden of his own inevitable failure.

—Locus

Rusch does a superb job of making the Retrieval Artist books work as fully satisfying standalone mysteries and as installments in a gripping saga full of love, loss, grief, hope, adventure, and discovery. It is also some of the best science fiction ever written.

—*New York Times* bestselling author
Orson Scott Card

Readers of police procedurals as well as fans of SF should enjoy this mystery series.

—*Kliatt*

What links [Miles Flint] to his most memorable literary ancestors is his hard-won ability to perceive the complex nature of morality and live with the burden of his own inevitable failure.

—*Locus*

Part CSI, part Blade Runner, and part hard-boiled gumshoe, the retrieval artist of the series title, one Miles Flint, would be as at home on a foggy San Francisco street in the 1940s as he is in the domed lunar colony of Armstrong City.

—*The Edge Boston*

Rusch defines emotional and intellectual cores in her stories and then plots the most fruitful and gorgeously panoramic orbits around them.

—*Wigglefish.com*

Praise for
THE POSSESSION OF PAAVO DESHIN

The Possession of Paavo Deshin is a masterfully crafted story. Definitely don't miss this one.

— Tangent Online

A custody battle like no other, where every side has its own agenda. An engaging story, a title very apt.

— Internet Review of Science Fiction

Praise for
THE DISAPPEARED

Rusch has created an entertaining blend of mystery and sf, a solid police drama that asks hard questions about what justice between cultures, and even species, really is.

—Booklist

It feels like a popular TV series crossed with a Spielberg film—engaging…

—Locus

The Retrieval Artist Series:

The POSSESSION of PAAVO DESHIN

A RETRIEVAL ARTIST SHORT NOVEL

KRISTINE KATHRYN RUSCH

wMg
Publishing

The Possession of Paavo Deshin

Published 2012 by WMG Publishing
www.wmgpublishing.com
First published in *Analog SF*, January/February, 2010
Cover art copyright © Philcold/Dreamstime
Book and cover design
copyright © 2012 by WMG Publishing
Cover design by Allyson Longueira/WMG Publishing
ISBN-13: 978-0-615-69928-8
ISBN-10: 0-615-69928-6

WMG Publishing
www.wmgpublishing.com

The POSSESSION of PAAVO DESHIN

A RETRIEVAL ARTIST SHORT NOVEL

Paavo saw them in a corner of the playground, standing together like they always did, their backs to the Dome. Through the Dome, he could see the Earth, misty white, green, and blue, like a beacon to the great beyond. He believed in the great beyond, Paavo did.

People Disappeared there.

He was sitting alone on the fake grass that covered this section of the ground. He usually sat alone: the other children thought him strange. His vocabulary was big for a seven-year-old, and he thought about a lot of things no one else his age did.

Paavo's private school held both a recess in the middle of morning classes and an outside athletic instruction in the middle of afternoon classes. Most of the kids from his class were on the black part of the playground, jumping on some diagram, playing an ancient game the teacher was trying to make them learn. It required balance and coordination—tossing a stone on designated parts of the diagram, hopping toward it in a pattern, then bending over and picking it up without touching any of the diagram's lines.

That was the afternoon's exercise. The teacher had left the diagram up so they could practice in the morning and during lunch.

Paavo didn't want to practice. He didn't like running and jumping and trying to keep his balance. He liked thinking and watching and studying. He liked sitting because he could handle surprises better when he sat.

Surprises like seeing the Ghosts.

He glanced toward them without moving his head. They seemed unusually solid today. Usually when they appeared, they flickered or a part of them was clear, a part that shouldn't be.

Standing with their backs so close to the Dome, the Earth framed behind them, the Ghosts should have had blackness where their stomachs were or a bit of blue, white, and green behind their faces.

Instead, they looked almost real. They stood side by side. They held hands. The man was a little taller than the woman. He had black hair. Hers was red, like Paavo's.

Usually they wore pretty clothes. His were shiny black like his hair; hers were green to match her eyes.

But this afternoon, the man's clothes were gray, shapeless, making him look fatter than he had looked before. The woman's were brown and loose. The brown leached the color from her hair—or maybe that was the whiteness from the Earth, reflecting through the Daylight Dome, diminishing the red.

The woman smiled at him, and Paavo shivered.

She had never smiled at him before.

2

He made himself look away. The kids were laughing. Anya had fallen, her hands splayed behind her, her feet straight ahead, the stone only a centimeter or so away from her shoes.

"Stupid game," she said and rolled off the diagram.

Paavo glanced at the Ghosts again. They seemed closer. Their expressions had changed again, which was unsettling. In the past, when he saw them, they'd appear suddenly. Usually they'd be on the edge of his vision. But sometimes they loomed right in front of him, their faces as big as his was when he pressed it against the bathroom mirror.

When they appeared like that, they'd say something familiar. Like the man speaking softly: *You'll be fine, child. If you remain resolute, no one can harm you.*

Or the woman, her eyes glinting with tears: *Remember how much I love you. That's all that matters, in the end. Just the love.*

He tried to tell his mom and dad about the Ghosts when he was really little. They didn't understand. First his mom and dad thought he had imaginary friends. Then they thought he was getting messages through his links. He had had links since he was a baby, even though children weren't supposed to get links until they were school age.

His parents had blocked his links so that he wouldn't get "contaminated" by adult knowledge. But his links worked better than his mom and dad thought they did; they always had. That was one reason his vocabulary was so big—he could scan the public nets if he wanted to. He just couldn't send and receive messages.

The fake grass rustled. He turned. The Ghosts were right beside him. They stank of sweat.

The woman crouched.

Tears leaked out of her eyes. There were lines on her face he'd never seen before.

"Enrique," she said, her voice trembling.

He froze, like he always did when they were too close. He waited for them to go away. But they weren't going away.

Instead, she grabbed his shoulders, pulling him toward her. Her fingers dug into his shirt; her nails brushed against his skin.

She crushed him against the softness of her coat, and he shoved away from her so hard he tumbled backwards, like Anya had done.

"You're scaring him," the man said.

"No," she said. "He shouldn't be scared. Not Enrique."

She reached for him again. Paavo pulled himself backwards, away from her, then rolled and got to his feet. The man grabbed at him, fingers brushing Paavo's arm.

Paavo shrieked and ran toward the pavement. The kids had stopped laughing. They were watching him.

They were watching him run.

He felt wobbly and out of shape, terrified that the Ghosts had touched him. They had never touched him before.

He got to the diagram, but the kids were still staring behind him. Not watching him after all.

4

He turned.

The Ghosts were still there. Only they weren't standing hand in hand. The woman was leaning on the man. He had his arm around her. Her body was shaking.

Paavo could hear her sobbing from here.

"Do you see them?" he asked Anya.

"Those people?" she said. "Yeah. They're not supposed to be here."

"I know," he said, and this time his voice shook. "I know."

2

"IT'S A STARTLING BREACH OF SECURITY," SAID SELAH Rutledge, the Headmistress of the Armstrong Wing of the Aristotle Academy. She bustled through the corridors of the school, the cape she had slung around her shoulders flapping behind her.

Gerda Deshin struggled to keep up. She was a tiny woman with short legs. She could never walk as fast as the others around her, and it seemed worse somehow, as she followed Selah Rutledge.

Or maybe it was the panic in Gerda's belly. Someone had tried to attack Paavo. Her boy was supposed to be safe here. She and Luc had paid a premium to get Paavo the best education and the best security in the entire City of Armstrong.

And still, someone had broken into the school, come onto the playground, and touched her child.

Selah Rutledge flowed around children standing in the corridors. The classroom doors were open, but no one was inside. The classes ran in fifty minute segments, with ten minute breaks, so that the children could relax, play, laugh or take care of personal needs like going to the bathroom.

That had been one of the features Gerda had liked about the Aristotle Academy when she toured it two years ago. Right now, she hated it.

She didn't want any of the children to stare at her.

Just like she knew they stared at her son.

Paavo was special. He had one of the highest IQs ever recorded by the Armstrong School District. Like so many geniuses, he couldn't quite understand why others didn't learn the same way he did. He talked about things too advanced for other children to grasp.

Sometimes he talked about things too advanced for her to grasp.

Her husband Luc had stopped trying. He loved the boy, but Luc knew he would never be as smart as his son. Paavo intimidated him. Sometimes Luc would say, *Explain it for Daddy, Paavo. Put in extra sentences.*

Gerda understood Paavo. She had since she first saw him, waving his chubby fingers and making goo-goo noises as he looked into her face.

Her heart twisted at the memory. She had thought she could make him such a happy child. Instead, he was lonely and a little strange. It had been the heart-break of her life to realize that loving him wasn't enough.

Selah Rutledge turned down a final corridor, this one devoid of children. Gerda finally recognized an area. This was the administration section of the building. It also housed finance and some of the most sophisticated large computer systems she had ever seen.

Each of the Aristotle Academies throughout the Earth Alliance was linked to the other Aristotle Academies. The academies were designed with three types of students in mind: the very wealthy who could afford the best education for their child, no matter what the IQ; the very paranoid who felt their child was under constant threat and needed a full panel of security; and the extremely brilliant whose child needed more than upscale tutoring—he needed an individual program tailored to his particular needs.

Luc had found the Aristotle Academy. Luc was the paranoid one. But Gerda had known from the moment she held Paavo that he was brilliant. She had held a lot of babies, and never had one under four months looked at her with such intelligence and focus. He had to go through a large battery of tests, which were repeated each year until his third birthday, and each time, he tested higher than the administrators had ever seen.

Selah Rutledge opened the door to her office and there, sitting among the desks, chairs, and real potted plants, was Paavo. He looked tiny and frightened, his cheeks tear-streaked. He had his shoes on the chair, his arms wrapped around his knees, and Gerda knew without even being told that he had been rocking back and forth, trying to comfort himself.

"Baby," she said, opening her arms. He ran into them and held her so tight that she couldn't catch her breath.

"The Ghosts," he said against her stomach. "The Ghosts were here."

Selah Rutledge had pushed the door closed. She walked to her desk.

Gerda tried to extricate herself from her son, just so that she could breathe. Finally, she pried his arms off her mid-section and crouched, trying to create some privacy for herself and her son.

"The Ghosts?" she said, trying to keep the alarm from her own voice. She hoped she hadn't heard him right.

He nodded, then wiped tears from his face with the back of his hand. "They *touched* me."

She frowned. He hadn't spoken of the Ghosts since he was four. He used to shriek in fear at the oddest times, staring ahead at nothing. The shrieks had started when he was just a year old.

Finally, she got Paavo to tell her what he saw. He saw people he said. Ghosts. As he got older, he could tell her why he thought they were ghosts. They were like the creatures in stories. Fake. He could put his hand through them. They would vanish. Sometimes they flickered in and out.

Luc called them imaginary friends. Gerda said friends would not make a child scream. Luc said seeing things was normal for children; so was making things up.

While Gerda agreed, she also knew that children with exceptionally high IQs were vulnerable to a host of mental illnesses. So she had him tested. The doctors found nothing, but suggested that he might be experiencing ghost images from those links that had been installed when he was much too young.

The doctors had judged her as they said it, assuming she had put in the links. She didn't argue. It was too complicated—everything about Paavo was complicated—but it had worried her all the same.

"The Ghosts touched you," she repeated, hoping she had misunderstood him.

He snuffled and wiped at his face again. "They *smelled*. They called me Enrique."

A shiver ran down her back. She kept one hand on her son's shoulder, and stood.

Selah Rutledge was watching them with great concern.

"Did anyone else see these Ghosts?" Gerda asked.

"All of the children did," Rutledge said. "Some of the older kids ran for security. When security arrived, the couple was gone."

That shiver ran down Gerda's spine again. "It was a couple?"

"A man and a woman," Rutledge said. "Here. We have it on our security monitors."

Before Gerda could warn her off, Rutledge pressed something on her desk. A life-sized image of the couple appeared in front of one of the giant potted plants.

Paavo screamed and clutched at Gerda.

"Shut it off," Gerda said. "*Shut it off.*"

Rutledge did. Her face had gone gray. "I'm so sorry," she said. "I hadn't realized."

"Clearly," Gerda said. She held Paavo against her legs. He was trembling.

"They never would have gotten off the grounds with him," Rutledge said. "We have protections—"

"Those failed." Gerda stroked Paavo's hair. She would have preferred to have this conversation without him here, but she couldn't leave him alone.

"I'm sure we can find some kind of satisfaction," Rutledge said. "This is a one-time thing—"

"It had better be," Gerda said, her voice so cold that it chilled her. She didn't realize she had such a voice inside herself.

But Rutledge's excuses angered her. The headmistress was afraid of a lawsuit and terrible publicity, not the effect this was having on Paavo. In fact, since they had come into the room, she hadn't addressed Paavo once.

"I want copies of those security recordings now," Gerda said. "I want to know exactly how those people got onto this campus and what your school is doing to track them."

"We're investigating," Rutledge said in a tone that implied they were in no great hurry.

But Gerda was. "I want you to solve this in the next few hours, or so help me, I'll go to InterDome Media and tell them that my child was assaulted on the playground of the Aristotle Academy."

"There's no reason to go to InterDome," Rutledge said, her voice shaking. Gerda hated that wobbly sound. It meant that her assumptions about Rutledge were true; the woman cared only about the school's reputation, not what had nearly happened to Gerda's son.

Gerda held out her free hand. "Give me copies of the security footage."

Rutledge nodded, looking trapped. She touched a white area on the side of the desk, then removed several very small chips.

Gerda took the chips and pocketed them. Then she crouched, picked up her son, and cradled him against her as if he were three instead of seven. He was so long his feet hit her calves. But she held him anyway.

"Here's what I expect," Gerda said. "I expect the people who attacked my son to be arrested by the end of the day. I expect a detailed plan from the Academy on how you'll beef up security. And I expect compensation for my son's trauma."

"I can't guarantee an arrest," Rutledge said, her voice small.

"Then I can't guarantee that I'll keep this quiet," Gerda said. Her back ached. Her son was too heavy to hold like this.

She let herself out of the room, not because the conversation was done—it wasn't, not quite—but because she didn't want to set Paavo down again, not in that place.

She carried him most of the way down the administrative corridor before she had to set him down. Then she wiped off his face, smoothed his hair back, and kissed him on his cheeks. They were chapped. He had been crying hard.

"The Ghosts," she said. "Tell me everything you know about these Ghosts."

3

SELAH RUTLEDGE SAT AT HER DESK, HER FACE BURIED in her hands. Never, in all of her years as an administrator, had anyone shaken her up this badly. It wasn't just that Gerda Deshin and, more importantly, her husband Luc Deshin were among the most powerful people in the City of Armstrong.

It was also the fact that somehow people unknown had breached the academy's security. If it got out that two people—whoever they were; whatever they wanted—had somehow entered the academy's grounds and tried to grab one of the children, the academy had no future in Armstrong. And she would have no future in academia.

But what bothered her the most was that the child seemed to know who these people were. Paavo Deshin wasn't the most stable creature: He burst into tears at the slightest problem. But he was—by the numbers, at least—the most brilliant child this academy had seen, one of the most brilliant children to ever go through any Aristotle Academy anywhere in the Alliance.

The brilliant could be eccentric; she had preached that to her staff for years. She wanted to give children the freedom to think and to be. But she didn't want them terrified.

And that was the underlying emotion for her.

Terror.

Selah Rutledge took a deep breath, then smoothed her hands over her face. She sat up. She had already reprimanded her head of security. Others within the academy were trying to find out what went wrong.

She would consult with them shortly.

In the meantime, she would find out who these intruders were.

She used the academy's extensive computer networks, opening links and lines she usually only opened during the rare admissions process. She took the images of the intruders and ran them through an Alliance-wide recognition system.

The system ran silently, searching through millions of faces and forms. While she waited, she watched the security recording again, this time slowly.

The couple had somehow avoided most of the cameras until they reached the playground. They waited through two different recesses, immobile, watching, and then straightened when Paavo's class came outside.

The law enforcement database pinged her. She swung her chair to one side to find four three-dimensional images standing on her desk. They were holograms that looked like they had been taken decades apart.

The system had separated the images out by gender. The two women stood side by side, and the two men stood side by side. Even to her untrained eye, the people looked like the same, except older in the security recording.

A unisex voice asked her if she wanted to hear the history of these people. She didn't want anything on audio. She set everything to silence, and instead, read what was on a screen floating in front of her.

Ishani and Károly Grazian, convicted over six years before of crimes against the Savang. The Grazians Disappeared to avoid prosecution.

Disappeareds.

Rutledge felt her confusion deepen. Disappeareds did not come to Armstrong. It was one of the centers of the Earth Alliance. Every alien group that belonged to the Alliance went through here. The Port of Armstrong had some of the best security in the entire Alliance, and the recognition program she had been using was the same version the Port used.

If the Grazians had come through the Port, then they should have been arrested and taken to the Savang.

That was the basis of the agreements throughout the Earth Alliance. The treaties that had created the Alliance—the treaties that allowed the enriching trade that had made the Alliance the power that it was within the known universe—had come with terrible strings.

In one of the earliest treaties ever signed, humans had agreed to abide by the laws of whatever culture they worked within. So if the humans were working on a planet dominated by the Disty, then humans were subject to Disty law.

Which sounded good in theory, but had turned out to be terrible in practice. Aliens were called alien for a reason—some of their laws were completely incomprehensible to humans.

Corporations, which operated on various planets and with hundreds of different cultures, soon learned the drawbacks to the Earth Alliance agreements. Administrators and management staff refused to work in the most extreme alien cultures. So the corporations guaranteed their people an escape should they accidentally run afoul of alien laws—particularly alien laws that humans found inane or nonsensical.

And so the Disappearance system was born.

The problem with it was that everyone who Disappeared was guilty of some crime. Some of the crimes were minimal by human standards, but that didn't matter. They were severe by the standards of other Earth Alliance members.

In Rutledge's eyes, as well as in Earth Alliance law, the Disappeareds were double criminals. They committed the original crime and then they compounded it by running away and assuming new identities.

She thought for a moment. The presence of the Grazians raised more questions than it answered, questions her security team wouldn't be able to handle.

She could hire a detective, but that was always iffy work. Besides, there were two kinds of people on Armstrong who specialized in the Disappeareds: Trackers, who didn't care how they found the Disappeareds, bringing them back to the authorities who had initially charged them, and forcing the Disappeareds to serve their sentences; and Retrieval Artists, who were a lot more subtle.

Retrieval Artists could find Disappeareds, but didn't return them for prosecution unless the person who hired the Retrieval Artist wanted that.

The Grazians had already risked arrest by returning to Armstrong. They were clearly cunning and able to break security protocols.

What Rutledge needed was a Retrieval Artist.

And she knew just the one.

4

PAAVO COULDN'T STOP CRYING, AND HE NEEDED TO. He had to stop being a baby so he could help his mom.

She wanted him to tell her about the Ghosts.

He stood in the hallway of the school, his mom crouched in front of him. She had that worried look on her face, the one that meant she was only a half-step away from panicking and calling his dad.

His dad never understood him. His dad would peer at him with that little frown, and then he would consult with Paavo's mom, and they would come up with something weird.

"Paavo," she said, "I really do need to know about the Ghosts."

"They touched me," he said.

"I know," she said. "You told me."

And he'd told her that they smelled. He didn't tell her that their clothes had texture, like real clothes, and he heard the woman's shoes squeak as she crouched.

"They're real," he said.

"I know that too." His mom used her *I believe you* voice, not her *maybe you believe that but it's not true* voice. Her *I believe you* voice calmed him like nothing else had.

"You know?" he asked.

She nodded. "Everyone else saw them too."

His eyes filled with tears again, but he couldn't cry. Babies cried. He wasn't a baby, no matter what the other kids called him.

She must have been worried that he was going to cry again, because she said, "These Ghosts, did they look different from the Ghosts you usually see?"

"Their clothes are different," he said. "Their hair is different. They're *old*. They smell."

"So they are different," his mom said. "But it's a man and a woman, right? Just like the first Ghosts?"

"They are the Ghosts," he said. He hated it when no one understood him. She asked if they *looked* different. They did. But she hadn't asked if they were different people.

"I know," she said. "But what makes them Ghosts instead of strangers who somehow got into the playground?"

They *were* strangers who got into the playground. But they were Ghosts too. If he said that, though, his mom would get really frustrated with them.

"They are *the* Ghosts," he said. "The same people who are always there. They're just dressed different and they got old."

The warm look faded from his mom's face. For a second, he saw real fear. He wasn't sure he'd ever seen fear on his mom's face before, but he must have because he recognized it and how would he have recognized it if he hadn't seen it before?

"They're the same people?" she repeated. "Only older?"

He nodded.

"And they're real." She glanced around like she expected someone to be standing near them.

Only no one was. It was just him and his mom in this hallway. No one else.

"Did they talk to you?" she asked.

He nodded.

"Did they call you anything?"

"What they always call me," he said.

That fear on her face, it had gotten worse, like she didn't want to hear what he had to say only she knew she had to.

"What do they always call you?" she asked.

"Enrique," he said.

She closed her eyes. Just for a moment, but that was long enough. For that moment, his mom was so scared she was afraid to look at him.

He knew what she was going to say before she opened her eyes and said it. She was going to say, *We have to talk to your dad*.

She opened her eyes.

Paavo braced himself.

She said, "Let's get you home," and her voice wobbled.

It was the wobble that scared him. The wobble and the fact she didn't want to go to his dad. She wasn't doing the normal thing.

And that scared Paavo most of all.

5

THE PING STARTLED MILES FLINT. HE WAS STANDING in the back room of his office, resetting the environmental system for the fifteenth time in twenty days. He would have to pay for an upgrade which he didn't want to do. He was trying not to work right now, so the expenditure irritated him.

When his fourteen-year-old daughter Talia heard that, she had called him cheap. *You can afford the upgrade, Dad. You can afford anything.*

He couldn't afford *anything*, but he certainly never had to work again if he didn't want to. He had structured his entire business so that he didn't have to work. He had learned early that Retrieval Artists shouldn't be beholden to anyone. They should be able to walk away whenever the job endangered the Retrieval Artist or, more importantly, the Disappeared.

So far, he had managed to live up to that. He had also managed to only take jobs that interested him.

The ping sounded again.

He shook his head in irritation. A client outside the door caused the ping, and right now, he didn't want clients.

The last case he had taken had put Talia in danger, and he had vowed not to take cases until she was no longer living at home.

But his curiosity got the better of him.

He walked into the main part of his office. It was a small room, unprepossessing by design, with a desk and a single chair. The walls looked like they were made of ancient permaplastic, even though he'd replaced the interior years ago.

He wanted clients to feel uncomfortable in here. The more uncomfortable they were, the less likely they were to hire him. He wanted to weed out clients anyway he could.

The security system had come on. A two-dimensional image of a woman standing outside his door over his desk. She wore some kind of cape, her hair mussed, her face turned away from his external cameras.

Still, she looked familiar.

Behind her, he could see bits of the neighborhood filtering in through the camera. His office was in the oldest part of Armstrong—the part that had first been settled—and his building was on Armstrong's Register of Historic Places.

The woman turned her head back toward the camera, and Flint blinked. He *did* recognize her. It was Selah Rutledge, from his daughter Talia's school.

Now his curiosity was aroused, which bothered him. He should have left the ping unanswered, but he wasn't going to.

Instead, he pressed the small corner of the see-through screen that unlocked the door.

"Come on in, Selah," he said as the door clicked open.

She looked startled. She stepped inside, trailing Moon dust with her. The ancient dome in this part of Armstrong never worked properly. Parts leaked, and one of the worst leaks was the never-ending dust that was part of the Moon's exterior.

"Miles," Selah said as she closed the door. "Normally, I wouldn't come without an appointment, but I have an emergency."

She looked flustered—and as long as he had known her, Selah Rutledge had never looked flustered.

"I'm not the person to come to for an emergency," he said. "The police handle those better than I do."

"Mine involves a Disappeared." She looked around for a client chair, failed to find one, and crossed her arms. Usually that movement pleased Flint but this time, it didn't.

He liked Selah. She was harsh, but she was a good administrator, and the Aristotle Academy had managed to take his too-smart, headstrong daughter, and make her into a successful—and more importantly—engaged student.

"An emergency involving a Disappeared?" he asked, all business now. "Someone you need to find?"

She bit her lower lip, then shook her head as if she were having a debate with herself. "I shouldn't tell you this. Your daughter is one of our students. But I couldn't think of anyone else to go to."

"Something went wrong," he said.

Selah nodded.

He didn't like the idea of something going wrong at the Aristotle Academy. To hide his unease, he said, "Let me get you a chair," and walked into the back. He grabbed the only other chair in the place and carried it back to the main room.

Selah was pacing. She stopped when she saw him.

"So what happened?" he asked. "Why do you need to find this Disappeared?"

It wasn't, as he quickly learned, *this* Disappeared. It was a pair of Disappeareds, a married couple named Grazian. They had fled Armstrong six and a half years ago, and now they were back and, oddly, they had somehow breached Aristotle Academy's security system.

Selah paced as she talked. She was as upset as he felt. He had taken Talia to Aristotle not just for their excellent academics but also for their security. He knew that he had enemies, and he didn't want any of them to get to his daughter.

But he also knew that the best security systems in the known universe could be breached.

He knew that because he had breached more than a few of them himself.

"Do you know what they wanted?" he asked.

"One of our students," she said.

A chill ran down his spine. But he made sure that he didn't let his unease show on his face.

"Any particular student?" he asked.

"Paavo Deshin," she said.

"Is that Luc Deshin's son?" Flint asked.

She nodded, looking somewhat sick.

He would have looked sick as well. Luc Deshin was the closest thing to a high-end criminal that existed in Armstrong. Many corporate CEOs skirted the law here, but Deshin actively flaunted it. He had a bevy of lawyers and a lot of money, and so far, no one could track anything to him.

No wonder his son was going to Aristotle.

"Do you know why these people Disappeared?" Flint asked, thinking maybe they were part of that very small group of real criminals who had violated laws that offended humans.

"Something to do with the Savang," she said. "I didn't look up anything else. When I saw that they were Disappeareds, I knew they would be hard to find, so I came to you."

He narrowed his eyes so that she could see his skepticism. "You came to me because you don't want to risk police involvement. You don't want anyone to know that the Aristotle Academy is vulnerable."

"That's true," she said.

"What do I do if and when I find these Disappeared?" Flint asked.

"Tell me," Selah said. "We'll take it from there."

He sighed. He hated cases like that. "No. I need to know what will happen to these people if I bring them to you."

"Are you asking me if we'll give them to the Savang?" she asked.

29

"Among other things," he said.

"I don't know what we'll do. Mostly I want them watched. I need to know why they're after Paavo Deshin and what exactly is going on."

"So ask Luc Deshin," Flint said.

"His wife has already threatened me," Selah said. "She wants to know who these people are."

"I'm sure her husband can find out."

"I'm sure he can too." Selah sighed. "I want someone I can trust, whom I know will do the very best job, not just for me but for the Academy."

"You'll make sure that Paavo Deshin is protected?" Flint asked.

"His family is already doing that," she said. "They won't let him back in school until this matter is settled."

Flint nodded. He would be the same way. "What about your other students? Are they protected?"

She gave him a sharp look. She knew he was asking about Talia.

"My security team is looking for the loopholes in the system. They promise me they'll be closed tonight." She sounded distracted as if that were the least of her concerns.

They were the greatest of his. "Let me look as well."

Her lips thinned. "That's irregular, Miles."

"This entire case is irregular, Selah," he said. "Besides, I have more experience with exotic security than anyone you could have hired."

She sighed again, then reached into the pocket of her cape. She removed several small chips. "This is the security footage from every angle. I even brought the audio from the moment that we learned of the breach."

He felt muscles in his shoulder relax. She was going to let him examine at least part of the system. If he could, he would convince her to let him examine all of it.

"What about your computerized systems?" he asked.

"What about them?" she asked.

"Most breaches aren't physical. They're cyber. Something gets shut down off-site and then your perpetrators get in. Often they're set up to be recognized as normal employees of the academy."

"Oh," she said. "I don't know anything about this."

"Give me access to your computer systems," he said. "I can figure out what happened."

She studied him for a long moment. "You seem to have a lot of skills, Miles."

Most people didn't know his rather checkered history—and he usually didn't have to explain it. But he did here.

"I used to design security systems before I became a police officer. Then, before I became a detective, I designed the Armstrong Police Department's security."

"And you quit all of that to become a Retrieval Artist," she said with the first hint of amusement.

"I quit all of that to become my own boss," he said. "Normally, I wouldn't take this case. I'm trying not to work until Talia's grown."

Selah nodded as if she understood. "You're taking this because of her."

"Absolutely," he said. "I need to be reassured that your system is safe."

Selah sighed. "That I do understand. And you understand why I don't want this out."

"I'm not going to broadcast to anyone that the Aristotle Academy has a vulnerable security system," he said. "You and I can agree on that."

"Are there other things we need to agree about?" she asked.

"Price," he said, "my rules for taking cases, and what you want from me."

"It sounds like a lot," she said.

"That's why I brought you the chair." He swept his hand toward it, indicating that she should sit down. "We have some talking to do."

6

GERDA STOPPED, HER HAND RESTING ON THE doorknob. She had the door to Paavo's room cracked open. It wasn't quite dark inside—Paavo hated full dark—but it was that strange sepia color that the Dome mechanics called Dome Twilight.

Her boy was curled in a fetal position on his bed, his arms around his stomach, his face pressed into his pillow. It had taken him nearly twenty minutes to calm down once they had come home, and then he had fallen asleep.

She hoped he slept for hours. She needed some time to herself.

She left the door open just a crack, so she could hear him if he cried out.

She took the security vids into the living room and used one of the separate computers Luc kept around for emergencies. The chips slid in as if they were made for the new system, and the images floated in front of her in holographic form.

She modified them so that they would be on a flat screen. She didn't want Paavo to wake up, come into the living room, and see his Ghosts yet again.

But she felt like they weren't his Ghosts any longer. They were hers.

Over the years, she had tried not to think of them: Ishani Grazian, her face red and blotchy, her eyes wet with tears; pasty Károly Grazian, his hand on her arm, leading her away as if they were going to their doom.

Gerda shouldn't have seen them. She had gone to the baby wing of the Child Center, her steps light, her mood even lighter. She had stopped just outside the door, about to enter when she realized something awful was going on inside.

The attendant had just taken a baby from Ishani Grazian. Only Gerda hadn't known that was Ishani at the time. She hadn't known anything. Just that an unhappy couple stood inside, unwilling to relinquish a child.

It wasn't until the couple left that Gerda realized the child they relinquished was hers.

Her Paavo.

Gerda had thought of that moment a hundred times over the past six years—the way Ishani Grazian had turned to her husband, his arms enveloping her, his face still turned toward the baby boy that the assistant carried out of the room. The couple had stood there for maybe five minutes, Ishani with her face hidden, her shoulders shaking as she sobbed; Károly with his head turned, his gaze on the closed door at the back of the family room.

That was what the Child Center called that room— the family room. Gerda had liked the name when she first heard it. Later, she had wondered at the wisdom of it.

That afternoon, she had stayed back, waiting for the couple to leave. Their distress was palpable, even through the clear window to the hallway.

Finally Károly Grazian said something to his wife. She raised her head, wiped her face with her thumb and forefinger, and nodded at him.

Then he put his arm around her and led her from the room.

They stopped just outside the door. Ishani Grazian looked directly at Gerda. Ishani's eyes were a bright green—brighter than any eyes Gerda had ever seen before. That unnerved her, and so did Ishani's expression.

Gerda had never seen such complete despair.

Not before—and not since.

Sometimes she thought it was the despair that caused the memory to surface so often. She hadn't understood despair then, but she understood it now.

She felt it whenever she looked on her son and thought about all the dangers he could face—not just as a brilliant and socially maladjusted child, but also as an adult living in a strange and hostile universe.

Not to mention the problems he would face as Luc Deshin's only son.

She had contacted Luc through her emergency links. He knew what was going on.

She hoped he would be home soon.

Gerda sank into her favorite chair and looked at the ever-changing wallscape. She had designed the images to soothe—water rushing down a cliff face in Vekke; the sun rising over a lake on Earth; the barren brownness of an unsettled portion of the Moon—but she barely saw them now, noting only as the images blended, one into another.

Normally, she would let Luc handle this. The Grazians and people like them were usually his problems. She didn't want to know.

But she couldn't let him handle the Grazians. She needed to know each and every detail.

She needed to keep those horrible people away from her son.

7

LUC DESHIN SLID HIS CHAIR AWAY FROM HIS DESK. The clear wall he used to screen flat images had frozen on two faces he thought he would never see again: Károly and Ishani Grazian.

Usually Luc forgot names. Especially names of the Disappeared. They had, for all intents and purposes, ceased to exist. So he ceased to think of them.

Yet these two had returned just like the nickname his odd little son had given them. They had reappeared like unwanted ghosts.

Luc's office was on the top floor of one of downtown Armstrong's few highrise buildings. His business occupied the floor below. His office rose above that, a bubble on the roof of the highest building in town.

That bubble gave him a spectacular three-hundred-and sixty-degree view of the city, the Dome, and the Moon beyond. He could see for kilometers.

Sometimes, he liked to say, he could see his entire empire, even though what he had wasn't technically an empire. It was a confederation of businesses, friends, and enemies, a grouping held together by the force of his personality and the power of his money.

What irritated him this time was that money wouldn't solve the problem he found himself in this very afternoon.

Gerda had sent him all of the information she had through an encrypted link. At his urging, she had told him what she knew, and then she had begged him to come home.

His Gerda did not beg. She was a strong woman, his equal in all ways. But this had upset her.

And, if he was honest, it upset him as well.

Not the least of it was Paavo. The child was inexplicably odd, impossible to talk to, and deeply loving. Luc's heart twisted whenever he thought of the boy. Sometimes, when Luc got home at night, he just enveloped Paavo in his arms.

He couldn't talk to the boy, but he could hold him, and that was enough.

It always made Gerda smile. *If only your enemies could see you now,* she would say. *They would know that everything they say about you is not true.*

But he was glad they thought it was all true. Because they said he had no heart. If they discovered his heart held his wife and son close, they would threaten his family.

Like the Grazians had.

He couldn't remember the last time he had felt fear.

Gerda had asked him to come home because she had felt the same fear. She wanted his presence to protect them.

But he knew a better way to protect them. He would send a security team to the house. Then he would get his number one in here and talk to him about finding the Grazians.

Finally, he would visit his lawyer.

The first measure protected his family should the Grazians be even bolder this afternoon than they were at the school. The second—if it worked—would ensure that they would never bother his family again.

And the third would take care of legal dctails he should have finished years ago.

He pushed one palm against the other, feeling the muscles in both arms strain. Once his life had been a lot easier. Once his fists had taken care of everything.

But that was long ago.

Before Gerda.

Before Paavo.

Before Luc learned that power exerted behind the scenes was always so much more effective than power exerted with two bruised and bloody fists.

8

Flint sat in the security room of the Aristotle Academy. Already he hated their system. The single room with no out-of-building back-up was too vulnerable to attack; they needed redundant and overlying systems.

He ran through the security protocols three times, and didn't find a breach—even though there clearly had been one. At first, he thought he was overlooking something. And then he remembered what he had told Selah: that many breaches came from outside hacking that changed internal protocols.

Unlike most security engineers, he knew how to search for a subtle outside hack. Someone who had gone through a backdoor, pretended to be a designer, and changed the system.

But he still found nothing.

Which made him rethink his entire approach.

There was a fool-proof way to break into a secure facility: Have someone on the inside let you in.

He searched for that and found no evidence of it. No one had let the Grazians in. They had walked through like everyone who belonged here.

Everyone who belonged. He looked through the system, to see what the protocols were to determine who belonged.

Nothing had been changed. There was nothing unusual. So he went back to the Grazians' entry to see how the security system had classified them.

And he started when he saw the answer.

It had classified them as parents.

Parents had access to all areas of the school except the administrative and security areas. They were allowed through the internal security systems by touching a scanner. It ran the DNA. A secondary protocol compared the DNA to their child's.

The system was different if the child was adopted. But most of the children hadn't been. So the system worked most of the time.

Flint back traced everything, and when he was sure of his information, he summoned Selah. Then he leaned back to wait for her.

The Grazians probably hadn't even tried to break through the system. They probably hadn't realized that the Aristotle Academy had a high level of security.

They had just walked through the front gate—as if they belonged.

Which their biological profile said they did.

9

Paavo woke up in near darkness. His heart was pounding and the skin on his face was stiff from dried tears. He wiped at it as he sat up, groggy from sleeping too long in the afternoon.

A woman sat at the edge of his bed. For a minute, he thought it was his mother. Then his eyes adjusted to the dimness.

It was the Ghost. The woman Ghost. The one who had grabbed him.

He didn't scream. This time she didn't scare him quite as badly as she had before. Maybe because he expected to see her again.

He wanted her and that male Ghost to leave him alone, but so far, they hadn't. And he had a hunch that unless his mom and dad did something to stop them, the Ghosts wouldn't ever leave him alone.

Paavo let out a quiet breath. He wasn't sure if she had seen him move yet.

Maybe if he thought it through, he could find a way off the bed and out of the room before she grabbed him again.

But he couldn't resist moving his foot toward her. As his foot got closer, he couldn't feel her weight on the bed, holding the covers down.

His heart beat even faster.

He kicked his foot toward her as hard as he could. He almost fell off the bed when his foot went through her image.

She still didn't notice him. She wasn't real then.

He blinked, saw that she was wearing the clothes she always wore, and her hair was its normal red. He flicked the lights on, and she turned toward him.

Somehow that movement had told her he was awake.

"Enrique," she said. "I'm so sorry we scared you. I didn't think we would. I thought we had been preparing you for the day we came back."

"You're not real," he said.

"I'm real," she said. "But this image isn't. It's a projection through some special links your father installed before we left. This visual of me is old, but the words I'm speaking are happening now."

"You're talking to me?" he asked. "From where?"

"That doesn't matter," she said. "What does matter is that we regain your trust."

"I want you to go away," he said.

"Enrique—"

"My name is Paavo," he said.

"Your given name is Enrique," she said.

"*My name is Paavo.*" He wasn't going to talk to her if she didn't call him by his real name.

"Paavo?" his mother called from the other room. "Are you all right?"

No, he wasn't all right. He was scared and confused and staring at the Ghost, only this time it wasn't real.

He took a deep breath to shout.

"Don't say anything," the Ghost said. "She can't see me. She won't even know I'm here."

He wasn't going to listen to any Ghost. No matter how much she scared him.

"Mooooom!" he shouted. "Mooooooooom!"

His mom came running. As she pushed open the door, the Ghost looked at Paavo. The expression on the Ghost's face was familiar. It was the sad expression she usually wore.

Only this time, it seemed like she was judging him too.

"The Ghost is here," he said to his mom. "She's sitting on the edge of the bed."

His mom looked directly at the Ghost. The Ghost shook her head slightly and then winked out.

"I don't see anyone," his mother said.

"She came through my links," he said. "She said she wanted to talk to me through my links."

"You don't have functioning links," his mother said.

"She said I do. She said my father put them in when I was little, before he left."

"Your father?" His mother was frowning now. She had come inside the room. She put her hand on the edge of the bed, right where the Ghost had been. "Your father doesn't know anything about links."

And then his mom got that scared look again, the one she had had in the school.

"Then what did she mean?" Paavo asked.

"She meant that they violated the agreement," his mom said. "Those bastards. They violated our agreement."

10

"IT'S IRREGULAR," SAID MÁIRTÍN OBERHOLTZ. "NOT to mention dangerous."

Luc Deshin bit back his irritation at the younger man. Máirtín Oberholtz had inherited his seat in the family law firm from his father, Martin Oberholtz. Luc had hired Martin fifteen years before. Luc had liked the old man. He was crusty and blunt and had a willingness to bend the law to see how far it would break.

Máirtín had no such willingness. Had this case been even slightly bendable, Luc would have demanded that Máirtín's father join them.

But this was a straightforward request, and Máirtín would fulfill it, whether he wanted to or not.

Luc put his hands behind his back and walked away from Máirtín's desk. He walked to the windows, wondering why there were curtains and why they had been pulled in the middle of the day.

The office itself was decidedly old-fashioned, with a lot of little niceties that had nothing to do with practicality and everything to do with ostentatious displays of wealth.

"The problem," Máirtín was saying, is that you are letting the entire city—hell, the entire universe, know that Paavo isn't your biological child."

Maybe it was time to find another attorney within the firm. Old Martin was doing less and less work, and Máirtín was too conservative for Luc. Had he known that Luc had ordered his security team to take care of the Grazians no matter what, he would have been appalled.

Even though Luc could argue that it was well within the law to go after Disappeareds when they reappeared. No court in any part of the Alliance would punish him for going after the Grazians. And if something went wrong, well, then, so what? It was the cost of doing business.

"My son knows I love him," Luc said.

"But people will wonder why you are adopting him now. Why did you wait? They'll talk—"

"So?" Luc turned slowly, keeping his body rigid. Máirtín started. He looked small behind his big black desk, like a child playing dress up in his father's office.

"So it wouldn't be good for the child," Máirtín said.

"It wouldn't be good for the child to have his biological parents steal him away in the middle of a school day," Luc said, "which is exactly what they just tried to do. I can charge them with kidnapping whether or not I adopt my son. But a court will look on me much more kindly if I fulfill the legal formalities. Right?"

Máirtín sighed. "A court is going to wonder why you waited—"

"I waited on the advice of your father," Luc snapped. "Paavo's parents are Disappeareds. They abandoned him. Your father felt we might get into messy Disappearance issues if I tried to adopt him while they were gone, living their brand new life. But they're back now, interfering with my family, and so I'm going to protect my family."

He paused, then leaned forward, placing both hands flat on Máirtín's desk.

"Think I'm going to have problems now?"

Máirtín's face reddened. "Um, no."

Luc had had enough. "I want one of your family law attorneys to handle this. I want the best you have, and that clearly is not you. Understood?"

"Yes, sir," Máirtín said. He sounded relieved.

"I want this done as soon as possible. If you can have it done within the week, great. If you can have it done by the end of business, even better. If I have to pay to get a judge to look at the petition before midnight tonight, I will."

"I doubt any judge will act that swiftly," Máirtín said.

Luc permitted himself another small smile. "Maybe not for you," he said. "But I'm sure one or two of them will roust themselves for me."

11

Before he left the Aristotle Academy, Flint gave Selah a hastily compiled bid to redo her security system. He knew she would hire him to do so. The fact that the Grazians had just walked in without a security check through a logical loophole in her system had unnerved her.

He had gone back to his office to research the Grazians. Normally, he would have done the research throughout Armstrong, using public systems and secure databases in several of his various haunts, always covering his tracks.

But since the Grazians had already made a very public appearance by trying to remove their biological child from his school, Flint felt no qualms in doing the kind of research that anyone would do—the kind that would usually send Trackers and alien governments after the Disappeared.

The court cases filed by the Savang against the Grazians told their personal history as well as the history of the complaint.

Károly Grazian had been a link engineer for ImaginaLink. He was paid to design new and different uses for the tiny chips that everyone had installed within their bodies. Some of the links were simply for communication, but others specialized—embedding cameras in fingertips, or adding taste buds for items humans couldn't normally taste.

Ishani Grazian had worked in customer relations for the same firm. She had marketed new and old chips to various consumer groups. Sometimes she found new ways to make old technology work for a particular group.

Six and a half years ago, the Grazians took a vacation to a major upscale resort on Sava, the home world of the Savang. The resort, Barrier Islands, catered to humans. Its brochures said it provided every possible amenity.

While there, the Grazians hiked along a mountain trail. Ishani lost her footing and fell five meters to a rock outcropping. The outcropping had only been one meter wide. If Ishani slipped again, she would have fallen forty meters to a valley filled with giant boulders.

She would not have survived.

Károly couldn't reach her manually, so he sent one of their companions for help. Then he unwrapped a thick vine from a nearby tree. He had Ishani loop the vine around her waist and pulled her to safety.

The parts of the vine that touched human skin died almost instantly. Some chemical native to human skin killed certain plants on Sava. The vine received a kind of toxin. The trees—and their vines—were sacred to the Savang, and destroying any part of them was punishable by death.

However, Savang law also provided that non-residents of Sava could buy their way free of a legal judgment by paying a set fee. The fee for freedom from a death penalty crime was more than two million credits.

The evidence against the Grazians seemed clear enough to convict them in a Savang court. But the Grazians and several other former vacationers at the resort brought a class action suit against the Savangs, claiming that the laws protecting the trees and vines were enacted only after the Barrier Island Resort was built. The trees, which grew quickly, were planted around the resort.

Further, the lawyers said there was no evidence in Savang history that the trees were sacred. The complaint the lawyers filed claimed that the Savang passed the laws, planted the trees and looped the vines near danger spots on trails—trails they could have closed off—with full knowledge that humans would touch the trees or vines, killing them.

The Grazians and the others in the class action suit claimed the Savang created the laws with the express purpose of extorting money from wealthy human clients of the resort.

The class action suit started as a stall to prevent the death sentence. But the Savang raised the stakes. They used an old law on their books which demanded that anyone who failed to pay a fine would have to do hard labor in a Savang work camp until the fine was paid or the appeals were settled.

The Grazians didn't have the money to pay the fine, and ImaginaLink wouldn't pay it for them. They faced years of hard labor in an alien work camp—which could kill them long before the appeals finished.

So they decided to Disappear instead.

Flint frowned as he examined all of this. There was no mention, in any of the court documents, of the Grazians' biological child. Was he at the resort? If so, where was he during the fateful hike? He would have been only six months old, unable to walk.

The questions bothered Flint so much that he stopped looking at the court documents and searched for any information on the Grazians' children. He found a seven-year-old birth certificate for one Enrique Grazian, whose parents were listed as Ishani and Károly Grazian.

He found no other information on Enrique. No images, no travel documents, nothing. Not even anything that established the Deshins as the child's guardians while the Grazians were gone.

Flint's stomach twisted. He hated loose ends, and this clearly was one. The Grazians were Paavo Deshin's parents. They had named him Enrique. He was born six months before the fateful vacation, before his parents Disappeared.

They clearly left him behind. Somehow the Deshins got him.

And now the Grazians had returned for him.

Flint's frown deepened.

The return was the key. The return and their carelessness about being identified.

Flint went deeper into the legal morass. His years as a Retrieval Artist had trained him to how to search through the legalese and find the nuggets of information he needed.

Still, it took him hours to figure out that the class action suit had been settled. It had not gone to any Multicultural Tribunal. In fact, when it looked like the case was actually going forward, the Savang proposed a settlement.

Most of the terms of the settlement were confidential, but a few were not. All charges against every single person involved in the suit were dropped.

Flint assumed that the remaining terms had to do with a financial settlement from the Savang to the humans. The Savang laws remained on the books of Sava, and nothing changed at the resort.

But the fact that the Savang were willing to settle out of court made him believe that the humans bringing the suit had been right: the laws existed only to trap aliens—in this case humans—who traveled to Sava for vacations. The idea was to bring money to the Savang—as a sort of legal extortion.

He shoved his chair away from his desk with a kind of low level anger. Had this all happened to him, he would not have settled the suit. Or if he had, he would have made sure a warning was one of his settlement conditions. Other humans had to know the risks they were taking when they went to Sava—particularly when they went to the Barrier Islands Resort.

He stood and paced. Something else bothered him about all that he had learned.

He still didn't understand the Grazians' actions. He understood why they Disappeared, although he didn't understand why they failed to take their child with them. Nor did he understand why they had returned for him over six years later.

Surely, they were bright enough to realize Paavo would have no memory of them. Surely, they knew that their presence in his life would be as disturbing as yanking him out of his tiny world and forcing him to Disappear. Maybe more so.

Flint went back to his desk. He probably couldn't find the answers he needed to the Paavo question, but he knew how to find Disappeareds.

And it shouldn't be that hard to find Disappeareds who no longer needed to hide.

If he couldn't figure out why the Grazians had left Enrique behind, he might simply go ask them himself.

12

Maxine Van Alen was sitting at her desk, tweaking an amicus brief that one of her legal assistants had prepared when the notice flashed across her links.

Someone wanted to adopt Enrique Grazian.

She stopped, closed her eyes, and rubbed three fingers across her forehead. In twenty years of practicing Disappearance law, no one had ever tried to adopt a child of a Disappeared—at least not without the Disappeareds' permission.

There was—as she always told her associates—a first time for everything.

She opened her eyes. Her desk sat in the middle of the room, but didn't dominate it. If anything, upon entering, the eye went to the conference table near the long windows. There were other desks as well, smaller desks that mostly existed for their separate computer access. Those computers weren't networked to anything within the law office, something she'd had more than one occasion to use.

The notification that came through her public links had simply flashed in front of her left eye. Like so many legal notifications, this was actually a notification of a notification. In other words, the message she got simply informed her to look at her daily inbox—the one set aside for non-specific legal cases.

When she got an assigned case, she set up an assigned mailbox within her own computer network. The Grazian case was so old that its mailbox had disappeared along with the clients.

If she had even set up a mailbox.

She often didn't for the Disappeared.

Van Alen helped people in trouble determine if they should Disappear. If she felt that they needed a Disappearance service, she pointed them to a good service, not one of the scams that had sprung up in recent years. She facilitated the distribution and/or (usually or) sale of assets, and because she was good, she made sure that the legal trail ended with her.

In addition to helping people Disappear to avoid such prosecutions, Van Alen and her team of lawyers also argued cases in front of more than thirty Multicultural Tribunals. The amicus brief she'd been reading was for an appellate case that argued these agreements with the alien cultures were not only inhumane, but illegal under centuries of human laws.

She had signed onto cases like that before or written briefs in support of those cases—and in all of those instances, her side had lost.

But that didn't stop her from trying.

Maxine Van Alen liked nothing more than an impossible task.

And she suddenly found herself facing one. The Enrique Grazian case presented all sorts of challenges. She slipped the notification language into any agreement that had to do with children of the Disappeared. When she first started doing the notifications, she wasn't even certain if they'd hold up in a court of law. Then when she realized that the chances of them being activated were slim, she stopped worrying.

But the worry came back the moment the Grazian notification crossed the lower corner of her left eye.

Because she would have to represent two Disappeareds in connection with their child. Only the Disappeareds had abandoned their lives and their identities.

They had given up their claim to legal status in this sector.

And she wasn't sure she could even revive it—not without some incredible legal gymnastics.

Still, she opened the file in her inbox and read the actual notification.

It was a standard document, stating that it fulfilled the terms of the foster child covenant by serving this timely notice to Attorney Maxine Van Alen of the intent of Luc and Gerda Deshin to legally adopt the child known as Paavo Deshin, a.k.a. Enrique Grazian.

Everything in the notification was in order. It was a competent legal document that followed every single requirement.

The only odd note came from the covering letter. The Deshins' attorney wrote: *I find nothing in the documentation in Paavo's files that links you to his case or his custody. We have fulfilled the notification request as we must do by law. That is the entire extent of our duties, so far as I can tell from this strange notation in Paavo's Foster Care Agreement. Unless I hear from you within 48 hours, this adoption will proceed as planned.*

Forty-eight hours was not enough time. Van Alen knew that without reviewing any files as well.

She immediately sent a request for an injunction against the adoption to the appropriate Family Court in the City of Armstrong as well as to Oberholtz, Martinez, and Mlsnavek, the law firm that represented the Deshins. Then Van Alen drafted a request for a closed hearing within six months time, claiming she could not put together all the needed information to block Enrique Grazian's adoption in a more timely manner.

She was careful not to use the boy's new name in her draft. She didn't want the name to slide through to future drafts. The Deshins' lawyer could claim that the use of the new name proved that Van Alen (and by implication, her clients) agreed with the merits of their case.

She wasn't sure what the merits were. She just needed the time.

Because right now, she was acting on behalf of Enrique's parents, who had Disappeared.

And she had no idea where they were.

13

GERDA WOULDN'T LEAVE LUC ALONE. SHE KEPT pinging his emergency links, and every time he asked her to talk to him on their private link, she refused.

She wanted him to come home.

Luc didn't want to go home—not while he was searching for the Grazians and had the new lawyer trying to push through the adoption, maybe that night.

But for the very first time in their relationship, Gerda wouldn't listen to him. She wanted to talk to him, and she wasn't going to do it through any encrypted channel. Nor was she going to drag Paavo to the office.

Not that Luc blamed her. The day's trauma would have disturbed even the most emotionally stable child. While Paavo was brilliant and charming and enjoyable, he was anything but emotionally stable.

Luc steadied himself as he walked through the front door of his own home. He had made sure no one followed him here. He had security planted throughout the neighborhood, not just bots, cameras, and warning signs, but some real human beings as well.

Right now, he had no idea what the Grazians were trying to do, but they weren't going to succeed in stealing his son.

The house always smelled faintly of mint, which Gerda had heard was calming, and usually, the scent worked. Usually, Luc smelled it, and smiled softly to himself, realizing he had come home.

But not this afternoon. This afternoon, his heart was racing, and he was breathing shallowly. As he stepped into the living room, he realized he was closer to panic than he had been in years.

He didn't want to lose any of this. He didn't want to lose his house or his family.

He didn't want to lose his son.

Before he called for Gerda, he looked for Paavo. He pushed open the door to the boy's room, expecting to see his son asleep on the bed. The covers were mussed, but Paavo wasn't there.

Luc's heart sped up. "Gerda?" he called.

She came out of the kitchen, a towel in her hands. Her lips were thin, and frown lines had formed around her mouth and eyes.

Luc had forgotten, until that moment, what a formidable woman his wife could be.

"It's about time," she said. "We have a very serious problem and we need to solve it now."

He didn't like her tone. She made it sound like he hadn't done anything all day.

"That's what I've been trying to do," he snapped. "If you hadn't demanded I come home—"

"If I hadn't demanded that you come home, then we would be in even more trouble," she said.

Something about her expression caught him. He had never seen that look on her face. "What's wrong? Did they get Paavo?"

"He's in the kitchen," she said. "He's fine."

But Luc had to see for himself. He hurried into the kitchen. Paavo was sitting in his favorite chair, his small, too-thin body hunched over the table.

He looked up and Luc winced at the sadness in his son's face.

14

SOMETIMES HIS DAD SCARED HIM, BUT NOT RIGHT now. Paavo heard his dad's voice from the living room, but didn't believe his dad was here until his dad burst into the kitchen. His dad was tall and athletic, the opposite of Paavo, and he was always so smart and so calm.

Only he didn't seem calm right now.

He hurried to Paavo and wrapped his arms around him, pulling him from the chair in a gigantic hug, so tight that it took Paavo's breath away.

"Daddy?" Paavo managed. "Are you okay?"

His dad eased Paavo back just enough so that they could look each other in the face. Unlike his mom, his dad could hold Paavo and not seem tired or winded, even though Paavo was getting taller and heavier by the day.

"Now that I know you are." His dad smoothed Paavo's hair away from his forehead. "I won't let anyone take you, you know that, right?"

Paavo did know that. Whatever his dad could prevent, he would. Paavo felt a relief so big that tears threatened.

His dad wiped at the bottom of Paavo's eyes. Clearly he'd seen the tears and this time, they didn't bother his dad.

"I know you're scared, Paavo," his dad said, "but we'll solve this. I promise."

Paavo nodded and put his head against his dad's shoulder, like he used to do when he was little.

"Thanks, Daddy," he said, and snuggled closer. "Thanks so much."

15

Luc held his son for a long moment. Paavo hadn't cuddled like this in a year, maybe more. Luc had started to wonder if his brilliant, difficult son was outgrowing him. At some point, Paavo would realize that his dad wasn't that smart.

Luc was just tough and determined. He liked having smart people around him, and he listened to them. He didn't always take their advice, but he listened. He knew how to take responsibility, he knew how to act, and he knew what he wanted.

Most people didn't know those things.

But his wife did. She came up to his side and put her hand on Paavo's back.

"We have to talk," she said to Luc.

He nodded, just enough to answer her, but not enough to disturb Paavo. He was about to carry Paavo to his room, when Paavo stirred.

"This isn't stuff you want me to hear, is it?" he said to his mom.

She sighed. Sometimes, she said, it was difficult having a precocious child. He understood too much and not enough at the same time.

"It'll be better if we can talk in private," she said.

Luc expected protests—that was usually how Paavo reacted—but this time, Paavo just nodded. He let go of Luc's neck, and let Luc set him down.

"Can I stay in here?" Paavo asked, and Luc suddenly understood that his son was afraid to go back to his room.

"Yes," Gerda said. "We'll shut the door."

Paavo returned to the table. He had been working some kind of puzzle there. One of the teachers had given him puzzles, not computerized things either, but very old fashioned, very expensive toys from Earth, saying that a puzzle of 3000 pieces or more would challenge Paavo's mind and rest it at the same time.

Luc let Gerda lead him out of the kitchen back to the living room. She pulled the door between them closed, and then, before he said anything, activated the sound-proofing.

"I don't think that's wise," he said. "I want to be able to hear if something happens to Paavo."

"I have set the security system so that it'll break through the soundproofing if there's even the slightest problem," she said.

"I'll monitor Paavo through my link to the house," Luc said.

She grabbed his wrist. "No, you won't."

He looked at her hand, small against his massive arm. That look would have intimated most people. It didn't seem to bother her at all.

"Károly Grazian installed links in Paavo," she said.

"We knew that." The links were tiny chips, put in much too early, so early that the bones had developed over them. The doctors claimed they could be removed, but it would be painful and possibly damaging to Paavo. "The doctors said they were inactive."

"They were wrong." She hadn't let go of Luc's wrist.

He wasn't even sure she knew she held onto him so tightly.

She leaned into him. "The Ghosts came through the links. They were programmed in. The Ghosts are the Grazians, Luc. They set up a program so that they could talk to Paavo. They've run programs ever since they left him."

He felt cold. "What kind of programs?"

"I don't know exactly. I'm just getting him to talk about them. But he remembers when we took him to the doctors. He remembers all that talk about the line between genius and insanity being thin. He's scared to tell us, afraid we'll think he's lost his mind."

Luc put his other hand over Gerda's and freed himself from her grip. Then he walked to his favorite chair. He couldn't quite bring himself to sit down—he was too nervous to sit—but he didn't like pacing either.

So he just grabbed the chair's back and looked out the window at the quiet street, the street he had thought perfect for raising children.

That had been his intent: raising *children* here, not just one child. But he had also wanted the smartest children he could get, and he knew that wouldn't happen biologically. He had some brains, and Gerda was smart, but together, they wouldn't produce brilliant children.

He knew it, and he knew it would be his fault. He investigated enhancements, but found out that they went wrong more times than they helped. The child—while brilliant early on—was prone to organic brain disorders which could be treated, but never cured.

He considered himself a risk-taker, but not that kind of risk-taker. He knew, because of his work, that there were a lot of children who ended up unwanted or abandoned. A few of them were babies, and he hired someone to test those babies. He wanted first choice of the brilliant ones.

Which wasn't quite how he found Paavo. His employee had heard about a couple about to Disappear. They needed someone to care for their son, who wasn't being pursued by the aliens.

The couple's delusional or very naïve, his employee said. *They believe they'll be back within the year. I know of no Disappeared who ever returns.*

Luc gambled on that, and took Paavo, who was stunningly brilliant—so brilliant that Luc abandoned the thought of raising other children. He and Gerda could barely keep up with Paavo. The boy needed their full attention from the moment he entered their lives.

"All the problems we've had with Paavo," Luc said softly, not looking at Gerda, "it's because of the Grazians?"

"We haven't had problems." She was always stubborn about defending that boy. Even though he was difficult, she saw him as perfect, the difficulties coming from his vast intelligence and nothing else.

"The emotional instability," Luc said. "His night terrors."

"Oh." Her voice was small, like it always was when he got her to admit there was something abnormal about Paavo. "Yes, I think those come from these links."

Luc nodded. "They did what, these two people? They tried to scare him?"

"I think they tried to keep themselves in his mind as his parents. But they have no idea how smart he is. He knows we're his parents. So the images confused him and scared him. And he knew very early they weren't real. So he thought he was making them up."

Luc's hand tightened on the chair top. His fingernails dug into the upholstery. The Grazians had terrorized his son for his entire life. And now, they were doing it in person.

"You could have told me this via our links," he said. He still wasn't looking at her. He didn't want her to see the expression on his face. His employees told him that when he got this way—cold and angry, calculating and vengeful—his face became something terrible to behold.

"No," she said. "I couldn't."

Something in her voice made him turn. Her expression was so flat that he had a hunch it mirrored his own. She was furious, just like he was.

Only furious was too mild a word. The coldness he felt—the coldness evident on her face—was something he would call a killing rage in his own private moments.

71

He had never seen his wife like this.

"I don't trust the links any more," she said. "Because this afternoon, Ishani Grazian showed up in Paavo's bedroom."

"What?" Luc said. "You should have—"

Gerda held up her hand, silencing him. "She showed up through what Paavo called her Ghost image—the old image—but talking to him in real time. His links are active somehow. Even though every test we ran says they weren't."

Luc frowned for a moment, about to ask why that mattered with his links, and then he remembered: Károly Grazian had designed links. Obviously, he had made the links specially for Paavo and knew how to activate them.

Who knew what else Károly Grazian could do with links. No wonder Gerda was being cautious.

"They told us that they were leaving his life for good," Gerda was saying, her voice tight and controlled. But Luc could hear the fury in it. "They told us that they wanted him raised by loving parents, that they didn't want him to live a life on the run. They told us that it was better this way."

She paused for breath, her cheeks red.

Then she said, "They *lied*."

He nodded. Lying wasn't as great a sin to him. People lied. But the Grazians had messed with his child's mind. With Paavo's brilliant mind.

And that was unforgivable.

"We'll be careful on the links," he said. "You start the research. We'll find the best doctors to remove those from Paavo. In the meantime, we'll find an expert to deactivate them."

"But right now, they can get to him," Gerda said.

"You keep him at your side," Luc said. "If he sees his Ghosts, have him tell you."

"What are you going to do?" Gerda asked.

He made himself let go of the chair back. "I'm going to make sure these people never interfere with our son again."

16

Hours of tracking the Grazians through the public cameras placed all over Armstrong. Flint had created a gigantic screen over the blank spot in his office floor. He had let the police program—one of many he had designed—search for the Grazians' features, tracing them as they moved from the port into the city, but he also insisted on watching the images, to make sure that the program hadn't given him false positives.

So far, he hadn't located where they were staying, but he knew he was close. He hadn't expected them to use their real names; that identity had been compromised seven years ago. He figured they were using their Disappeareds identities. It wasn't quite fair to call those identities new—they had had them for almost seven years now—but that wasn't how the two of them were known in Armstrong.

Finding out those identities would be impossible, at least through the usual channels. He never tracked Disappeareds through the new identity. If he stumbled on it, then he considered himself lucky. But so far, he hadn't stumbled on anything.

All he could say for certain was that they came through the port, traveled west once they left it, and a few days later, ended up at the Aristotle Academy.

A ping startled him. A new screen floated above his desk. Someone was outside his office—the second time in two days. And it wasn't just any someone.

It was Maxine Van Alen.

Flint frowned. He couldn't remember Van Alen ever coming to his office before. They had worked together on a number of projects—including one to bring down the largest law firm on Armstrong.

In all the years they'd worked together, Van Alen had never before come to Flint's office. She had always demanded he come to hers.

Her visit was so unusual that he had his system double-check her identity before he unlocked the door so that she could come inside. As she pulled the door open, Flint saved the programs he was working on, and compressed the screens.

Van Alen always looked stunning. On this day, she wore a black and white dress—the bodice white and the skirt black. Only the divider wasn't horizontal along her hips, it was a diagonal slash that ran from one shoulder to the top of the other thigh. She had colored her hair black to match the skirt, with a white streak that ran in the opposite diagonal from the skirt. She had also coordinated her eyes—her pupils were black with a single white slash going through them—as well as her fingernails. The entire effect made her seem exotic—or it would have, if it weren't for the Moon dust coating her black and white shoes, and her legs up to mid-calf.

Flint suppressed a smile. She hadn't noticed the Moon dust. She would be annoyed when she did.

"Maxine," he said as the door closed behind her. "To what do I owe this honor?"

"I need your services immediately," she said. "You're the only person I can trust with this."

He hated sentences about trust. They always made him feel obligated—and Maxine Van Alen was smart enough to understand that.

"What happened?"

"I have, of all things, a domestic," she said. "And it's happening fast. The other side has a judge in their pocket. We're due in court by eight tonight, and I can't seem to get a stay."

Flint shrugged. "I can't help you with court."

"I know that," Van Alen said. "But you might be able to help me find my clients."

Now he was intrigued. "Hold on," he said. He went to the back and got the chair for the second time in two days. He was beginning to think he should just leave it in the front room. He seemed to bend about providing it to clients anyway.

"I take it your clients are Disappeareds," he said as he returned.

"And someone wants to adopt their only child," she said.

He set the chair down, feeling the hairs on the back of his neck rise. She couldn't be working on the same case, could she?

"I'm pretty sure it's legal to adopt the child of a Disappeared," she said as she sat down. "Technically, if they leave a child behind, they have abandoned it. Especially since they've changed their identities, and fled punishment for a crime."

She noticed the moon dust on her skin and brushed at it. It clung to her hand.

"But," she said, "I have always put in the foster care agreement that if the foster parents want to adopt the Disappeareds' child, I receive notification of the intent to adopt. The theory is that the notification would allow me to contact my clients, the Disappeareds, and I would act on their behalf."

"You would search out a Disappeared because the people who raised their child wanted to adopt?" Flint asked.

"When I set this up," Van Alen said, "I thought I would make a valid attempt. Honestly, I did it to salve my conscience. These children already have a difficult life. I thought this might make things easier—particularly for the older children—if they knew exactly what their biological parents' wishes were."

"I can't believe a parent would leave a child behind," Flint said.

"I know you can't, Miles," Van Alen said, "but that's just because you can't see past your own circumstance. And if you had to Disappear because of some case, and for some reason, you couldn't take Talia, I'm sure you would provide for her. You might even find the right people to raise her or someone to adopt her."

He couldn't imagine the circumstance. But he hoped he would be that farsighted.

"Sometimes people leave overnight. They don't have time to take care of everything," Van Alen was saying.

"Finding a decent home for your child is not something you leave to the last minute," Flint said.

She shrugged. "Not everyone is like you. Besides, this clause wasn't important. It had never been activated, not in all of my years working with the foster agency or the Disappeared."

"Until now," Flint said.

"Until now." She folded her hands on her lap.

"You actually want to search out a Disappeared because someone cares for a child enough to make the relationship with that child permanent?" Flint asked.

Van Alen sighed. "I have an obligation to search them out."

Flint frowned, thinking of the images he had seen of Paavo Deshin, screaming as his biological parents touched him. "And if the child doesn't remember the Disappeared?"

"Oh, it's a mess, I know that," Van Alen said. "The entire Disappearance system is a mess. And that's what has me thinking."

Flint leaned back in his chair. Sometimes Van Alen overstepped. "Thinking what?" he asked.

"Normally, in cases like this," she said, "I would advise the Disappeareds to let the child go. There are a variety of reasons. Some are simple. The Disappeareds usually can't return for their day in court. They ran away to save their own lives. I would make a good faith effort to find them—maybe just a short search, confirming that they did indeed Disappear—and then I'd let the adoption proceed."

"But you're not going to do that in this case," Flint said.

"In this case," Van Alen said, "the Disappeareds have been cleared. They can come home. They can actually go to court and fight for their child."

Flint felt cold. This had to be the Grazian/Deshin case. Did she know he was already working on it? If so, how?

"The problem is," Van Alen said, "I have to find them immediately. I need them by tonight. If I know exactly where they are, and they can't get here by this evening, I have my grounds for a stay."

"You want me to find them," Flint said.

She nodded.

"Yet," Flint said, "you would normally advise them to stay put. You would tell them the child was already lost to them. What's different? They still chose to leave the child behind."

Van Alen gave him an odd look. "You don't approve of this, Miles?" she asked. "Why not?"

He waved a hand at her, forestalling this part of the conversation. "Finish telling me what you're thinking. This isn't about the Disappeared couple or their child, is it?"

Her eyes lit up. "There are several factors here. First, the family had to split up because the parents Disappeared. They didn't want to drag the child into a life on the run."

"So they thought it better to have the child raised by people they didn't know?"

"They had no idea how long they would be gone. They were in a class action suit against the alien government—"

"This is Ishani and Károly Grazian," Flint said.

Van Alen's mouth opened a little, and then closed. Flint had never seen her flummoxed before, but that was what he had done. He had flummoxed her.

"How did you know?" she asked.

"The details are familiar," he said. "I'll tell you why in a minute. Finish telling me why this is so important to you."

"Okay." She had to take a deep breath to gather herself again. "They didn't think they would be gone very long. They were set up. This crime—"

"I'm familiar with it," Flint said.

"Then you understand. Their Disappearance is even more sympathetic than most. And now that they won their suit, they can return home."

"That still doesn't explain why you're so pleased to have this case," Flint said.

Her eyes narrowed. "There are several factors. First, the adoption is coming now. Why did the foster parents wait? Secondly, one of the foster parents is well known in criminal circles."

"There's no proof that Luc Deshin is a criminal. Just that he has had interactions with criminals," Flint said, a little more primly than he intended. "*I've* had interactions with criminals. So have you."

"But we're not considered a conduit to Armstrong's underworld," Van Alen said. "Deshin is."

Flint sighed. "That's still not enough. What is it about this case that has you so motivated?'

"We will probably lose," she said. "But that's what I want. I want to appeal this all the way to the Multicultural Tribunals. This is the kind of case I've been waiting for. This case calls into question the entire system of treaties on which the Earth Alliance is based."

She would lose. No one had challenged the treaty system and won. At least, not yet.

But he couldn't make that argument. She would say that it only took one case to break down the barriers. So he tried a different tack.

"You're proposing something that will take years," Flint said.

Van Alen nodded.

"What about the child?" Flint asked. "He'll be in constant limbo. You'll ruin his life."

"What kind of life can he have as Luc Deshin's child?" Van Alen asked.

Flint frowned. He hesitated for just a moment, then he punched up the gigantic screen he had had up before. Only instead of the images of the Grazians he was culling from various cameras all over Armstrong, he called up the security footage from Aristotle Academy.

He focused it on the playground and kept the image of young Paavo Deshin in the center of the frame.

"This is Paavo Deshin," Flint said. "You know him as Enrique Grazian. And those people hovering in the back there, that's Ishani and Károly Grazian. They tried to kidnap the boy today. Watch his reaction to them."

Flint ran the images, but didn't look at them. The little boy's anguished face was already burned into his memory. That child's reaction was deeper than fear of strangers. Something about these people terrified him.

Van Alen swore softly. She crossed her arms and looked away.

"We don't know what caused that reaction," she said. "Maybe Luc Deshin told that boy that anyone who tried to take him away was going to kill him."

"Maybe," Flint agreed. "Or maybe Deshin is setting up the adoption today to make sure he won't lose his child to the Grazians."

"You don't like them, do you, Miles?" Van Alen asked.

"The Grazians?" Flint asked. "I don't know them. But the fact that they left that child behind bothers me. I see nothing in the record that tells me why they did. Their excuse is flimsy. They should have Disappeared with him."

Van Alen studied him for a moment. The image on the screen to her side had frozen on Paavo Dashin's terrified face. But she had turned enough in her chair so that she didn't have to look at him.

Obviously, his expression did disturb her, and she wasn't going to think about it. She thought her assault on the treaty system was more important than one young child.

"You're not going to tell me where they are, are you, Miles?" she asked.

"I don't know where they are," he said. "I've been trying to track them for hours."

"Track?" she asked, picking up on the word. She knew he hated Trackers.

"Yeah," he said. "The Grazians are no longer in any danger, so I figure there's no reason to be careful."

Her lips thinned.

"I'm working for the Aristotle Academy," he said. "They want to protect Paavo."

"I'd like to hire you as well," Van Alen said. "Maybe get you to speed up, find them quickly, and get them to court tonight."

He glanced at the image. The little boy had already wormed his way into Flint's heart.

"How can bringing them to court make things worse?" she asked. "It might settle everything."

"It might," Flint said.

"Luc Deshin is a criminal," Van Alen said.

"So, technically, are the Grazians," Flint said. "The court did not invalidate the laws of Sava. It just pardoned all of the people trapped in that cycle."

She stood. Her body blocked the image of Paavo's face. "I'm going to act in the Grazians' interests whether they come to court or not," she said.

Of course she was. And she might be able to get her stay. It wouldn't hurt to tell her where the Grazians were, if he could find them.

And he probably could by eight o'clock that evening.

"If I find them," he said, "I promise I'll let you know."

"But you won't contact them yourself, will you?" Van Alen said.

"All I've been hired to do is locate them," Flint said. "By the Aristotle Academy and now by you. You're still paying my full fee and expenses, by the way."

She grinned. "I wouldn't have it any other way."

She walked around the image. Then she stopped, her hand on the door.

"That child's future is really none of our business, you know," she said. "We should just do our jobs. Mine is to act in his parents' best interest. Yours is to find them. What happens after that isn't up to us."

Flint bit back his initial response. He just nodded, and said, "I know."

She smiled at him, as if she approved of what he said, and then she let herself out the door.

He sighed and sank into his chair, looking at Paavo Deshin's terrified face. If Flint had been the kind of man who believed in doing his job and nothing else, he would still be a police detective, a man who handed children like Paavo Deshin over to alien governments to answer for their parents' crimes.

Van Alen was right; the treaty system was unfair. Flint hated it too. But he wasn't willing to sacrifice one little boy's future to pursue a court case that might or might not change the way the universe worked.

If he found the Grazians, he would tell Van Alen so that the Grazians could show up to court. But he would show up too. And he would speak up if he felt it necessary.

The question was, what side would he step in for?

He still wasn't sure.

But, looking at Paavo's tear-streaked face, he knew who he would defend.

17

LUC'S PEOPLE COULDN'T FIND THE GRAZIANS. HE PACED his office, feeling frustrated, feeling pressured.

Feeling frightened.

These people had damaged his son. Now he would have to take the boy to specialists just to have those links shut down. Paavo hated doctors—Paavo hated anything outside of routine.

Luc used to think all of Paavo's tics came from his great intelligence. Now he wondered if the Grazians hadn't caused those tics, with their programmed contacts, the adult communications.

Luc shuddered. Part of him was relieved his people hadn't found the Grazians. For them to show up dead on this day, after all of the discoveries, after the contact with Paavo, would confirm what people had suspected for more than a decade:

There was a darkness to Luc's business. One he tolerated of necessity.

One he used when he had to.

Only he had never used it for personal gain. And while this wasn't personal gain, it was personal.

It was revenge.

Revenge and fear and all of those things he never admitted to. He wanted those people to pay for contacting his child. For hurting his child.

He wanted to hurt them back.

And he still might. But he wouldn't do so on this day. He had an adoption to finish.

That might be enough: An adoption, shutting off the links, repairing poor Paavo as best as possible.

Then again, it might not. Károly Grazian had designed links. What else had he put into Luc's son? What else could he trigger?

And why?

That was what bothered Luc the most. Why did the Grazians torment the child when they had given him up in the first place?

Luc continued to pace, unable to think about his work or anything else. Anything except these two horrible people and Paavo. Paavo's fear-filled eyes.

Luc clenched his fists. In the morning, no matter what the outcome of the adoption, he would hire a Retrieval Artist. He would find those two horrible people. Once he had their location, he would figure out how to take care of them.

He wouldn't threaten them. That was too unsophisticated. He wouldn't force them to leave Armstrong either, because they could still contact Paavo through modified links.

He would figure out a way to shut the Grazians down. And he would do it with cold calculation. Not this edge of panic.

He would make sure they never harmed his son again.

18

After Van Alen left, Flint continued his search for the Grazians. The program he had designed had followed them from the port to one of the older sections of Armstrong—although not as old as this section.

They had gone to a series of low-rent hotels, always coming out looking discouraged.

Even the lowest-rent hotels wanted some form of identification or a great deal of money. Flint glanced at the time stamp. All of this had happened four days before.

Before Van Alen had shown up, he would have gone to the hotels himself, figuring he had time to continue his search, maybe over a couple of days. He would have learned their new name or the barrier to staying in some of those hotels. He would have gathered a great deal of information.

But he didn't have that luxury. So he let the program continue, glancing idly at it as he conducted another bit of research.

This one was for him. He examined old hospital records, as well as records from the foster care system. He had already found Paavo's birth certificate. He wanted to find more. He wanted to see if the name Grazian turned up before they left on their so-called vacation.

It did. One of the local hospitals had a child-rearing program, and Ishani Grazian had registered for it. She specifically asked for a program for difficult children, which did not exist, although the program coordinator made note of it.

Ishani Grazian was referred to a mental health specialist. She was told he specialized in difficult children. He didn't; he specialized in inadequate parents.

Flint leaned back in his chair. How could a child who, at that time was only a few months old, be difficult? He had raised a baby from birth to toddler; all of them were difficult. Babies cried, and parents got no sleep. Some babies had health problems, which made the situation worse.

But Paavo—then Enrique Grazian—hadn't had health issues. He was a very healthy baby. But something had gone wrong.

The other program pinged Flint. He looked up. The trail had stopped at one of the low-rent hotels. He went back several hours and scanned through the images.

The Grazians had hurried to the hotel after leaving the Aristotle Academy. Ishani Grazian had been crying. Her husband cradled her the entire way, his arm around her.

Flint had the sense that Károly Grazian wasn't trying to stop her tears, but to keep her face away from the cameras.

He knew they had broken the law.

Flint examined all of the cameras around the low-rent hotel. He found no evidence that the Grazians had left. They were probably holed up inside, planning what to do next.

He sighed. He had promised Van Alen he would let her know that he had found them.

He had also made the same promise to Selah Rutledge.

He contacted both women, and waited for them to tell him what they wanted him to do next.

19

GERDA FED PAAVO A DINNER HE DIDN'T WANT, AND then made him dress in his best outfit. It was a blue suit with a long coat that made him seem taller than he was.

When he came out of his room in that suit, wearing his shiny shoes, his hair neatly combed, he looked older than he ever had.

She put an arm around him, pulling him close. He leaned against her for an instant, then straightened, trying to be adult.

She had already explained to him that he was going to go with her to court. They would have bodyguards so that no one could go after Paavo when he left the house. Still, she had been reluctant to take him out of this safe place, but Luc insisted.

The lawyer Luc hired figured it would be best if Paavo was there, so that the judge could see just how much the Deshins loved him.

He won't be some generic child, Luc said. *The court will see that he's our child. They'll see how special he is, and how much he needs us.*

Paavo slipped his hand in hers. He looked up at her. She gave him her best smile. She didn't want him to know how nervous she was.

Yes, they loved him. Yes, they had cared for him since he was six months old. Yes, they had given him the best life they possibly could.

But she knew what everyone in Armstrong said about Luc. He had been arrested half a dozen times, but he had never been convicted. He always stayed on the right side of the law, letting the people around him do the difficult work.

If the lawyer for the other side got any of those people to testify, things could go horribly wrong.

"Something's really bad, isn't it, Mommy?" Paavo asked, echoing her thoughts. Every time he did that, it unnerved her.

"Things could be better," she said. Then she noted that he had called her "Mommy," something he hadn't done in a very long time.

She hugged him again.

"But we'll get through it," she said to him. "We always do."

20

THE COURTHOUSE WAS A LARGE BUILDING IN Armstrong's City Center. There actually wasn't one courthouse but several, all of them attached to Police Headquarters or to the jail.

It always made Luc Deshin's heart speed up to go inside any of the courtrooms. He had been sixteen and in trouble the first time he had come here. Somehow, without a lawyer, he had talked his way out.

But that experience stuck with him. Every time he walked through the faux glass doors into the faux marble corridor, he felt sixteen again and out of his depth. This time, he had a pretty young lawyer beside him.

Celestine Gonzalez was the lawyer that Máirtín Oberholtz had recommended. Luc researched her and was pleased; she was young, but she had won every difficult case she'd been asked to handle.

Luc himself didn't intimidate her. When he had entered her office, already angry at Máirtín, she had smiled at Luc.

I see you've met the new boss, she said with a twinkle in her eye. That one comment had relaxed Luc. Her later analysis had calmed him as well.

You have a certain reputation in this town, she had said. *I am going to neutralize it. This case will be about the loving home you have provided for Paavo, and how that boy has thrived under your care. And from what I can tell, I won't be stretching any points. Before you got here, I spoke with the administrators of the Aristotle Academy. You have quite a special child there, one which they say couldn't be as special as he is without nurturing.*

She had flattered Luc and relaxed him at the same time. He only wished she could do the same thing now.

They had one of the family law courtrooms on the second floor. It had been designed in something called the Federal Style—all columns and faux marble and simple wooden-appearing benches, with a matching balcony. The judge's bench was high, with a witness stand to the right. The jury box—empty for this case—stood to the left. It had the most comfortable chairs in the room.

Luc and Gonzalez sat behind one of the tables up front. The other was reserved for the Grazians, should they show, or their lawyer. Gonzalez had already informed Luc that they did have a lawyer, and she was trying to slow down the proceedings, something he hadn't wanted.

Gerda hadn't arrived yet, which worried him. He wanted her here now. He had already checked with her—she had left just a few minutes ago. The bodyguards were with her. He had put his best men beside her and Paavo. He had robotic guards following, as well as a few of his seedier employees keeping the perimeter.

If the Grazians chose to attack his son on the way to the courthouse, they would never make it inside.

But Luc did know better than to go after them here.

The hearing was scheduled for eight sharp. It was a few minutes before, and so far, the Grazians hadn't shown up. Neither had their lawyer.

A slender man with curly blond hair slipped into the back. He had the palest skin Luc had ever seen and eyes so blue they seemed artificial. He nodded once, as if he knew who Luc was, then sank into one of the hard seats.

But no one else followed him inside.

"What if they don't come?" Luc asked Gonzalez.

"We make our petition, and we win," she said. "It'll be uncontested."

She had been facing forward. As she spoke, she glanced back at the door and saw the blond man.

"You didn't hire a Retrieval Artist, did you?" she asked Luc quietly.

"No." He didn't tell her that he planned to do so if the Grazians didn't show themselves this evening.

"Hmm." She smiled at the man behind them. "What's your interest in this, Miles?"

"I'm just an observer, Celestine," said the man in the back.

"Who's that?" Luc asked.

"A former client," she said. "And an excellent Retrieval Artist."

The panic rose inside Luc again and he had to let out a slow breath to knock it back. It didn't matter that a

Retrieval Artist was here. It didn't matter if the Grazians showed up. It didn't even matter if the adoption failed.

Luc had contingency plan after contingency plan. He would make sure that no one took his son from him.

Not ever.

21

GERDA CLUTCHED PAAVO'S HAND AS THEY HURRIED up the marble steps inside the courthouse. The place was empty, and that unnerved her. She turned to the guards who were a few steps behind them.

"Keep an eye out," she said.

For what, she wasn't certain.

Paavo was getting winded. She had to slow down so that he could keep up.

"I thought you said we were going to meet Dad." He gasped the words.

"We are," she said. "He's in a room at the top of the stairs."

Or so she hoped. She reached the top of the stairs and pushed open the double doors. To her relief, Luc stood at the front of the courtroom with a pretty dark-haired woman beside him.

She had to be the lawyer. She seemed awfully young to have their entire family's fate in her hands.

Paavo let go of Gerda and ran to his dad. He wrapped his arms around Luc, and to her surprise, Luc let him. Luc kept one hand on Paavo's head, holding him close, but looked at Gerda.

For the first time in her memory, her husband looked shaken.

"Is everything all right?" she mouthed.

He shrugged.

He didn't know. That unsettled her even more.

"All rise," someone said from the front. A man not too far from Gerda stood. He was blond and pale. She had never seen him before.

He was the only other person in the courtroom, and she knew he wasn't Károly Grazian.

"You and Paavo should sit behind us," the lawyer said.

Luc disengaged Paavo. Gerda hurried to the front and took her son's hand as the judge entered.

She was older than everyone in the room combined. Or she had enhanced herself to look that way. She had steel gray hair, a thin but lined face, and a pinched mouth.

Gerda's breath caught in her throat. She had to trust that woman? She didn't want to think about it. She put her arm around Paavo's shoulder and pulled him gently into the bench along with her.

Then the voice told them they could all sit down.

The judge gaveled the session to order.

"I'm scared, Mommy," Paavo whispered.

Me, too, Gerda thought. But she didn't say it. Instead, she gave her son a brave smile, took his hand, and prayed everything would go her way.

22

THE GRAZIANS WERE ALREADY TWO MINUTES LATE, which wasn't going to help their case with the judge. Maxine Van Alen had sent one of her associates to fetch them. The associate had contacted her to let her know that he had found them and they were coming to court—"gladly," he had said, although she was beginning to doubt it.

They should have been here by now.

If she didn't get upstairs in three more minutes, she would lose the case by default. Judge Connelly did not tolerate tardiness in her courtroom.

Van Alen had started for the stairs when the courthouse door opened. A couple hurried in, followed by her associate. The Grazians. She thought she had forgotten what they looked like, but the moment she saw them, she remembered—and shuddered ever so slightly.

She had loathed Károly Grazian. The man had been controlling, the kind of person who never listened to advice, and felt everyone's opinion was worth less than his own.

The entire case came back to her then—her arguments to the Grazians six and a half years ago that they shouldn't Disappear if they filed the class action suit, but if they did Disappear, they should not file the suit.

If you stay, you make a compelling argument for your innocence, she had said. *If you go, you should simply become brand-new people and not let the past hold you.*

They hadn't taken either bit of advice. She had given the class action suit to another lawyer, partly because she didn't want to fight for clients who refused to stick around and fight for themselves.

Ishani Grazian clung to her husband's hand. The woman irritated Van Alen more than the husband did. She did everything Károly told her to, especially when he told her that all of his ideas were for her own good.

"We have to get upstairs now," Van Alen said, "or we will lose by default."

She didn't wait for them, but started climbing the stairs. She had planned to discuss her entire strategy with them before they went inside the courtroom, but their tardiness made the discussion impossible.

As she opened the double doors, she felt a palpable sense of relief. She didn't want to discuss appeals or the treaty system with them. She didn't want to talk about spending years on this case.

Did that mean she wouldn't do the best job she could for her clients?

She hoped not.

She would still do the best she could. But she would do it all on her terms, not on theirs.

23

"So good of you to join us, Ms. Van Alen," the judge said.

Flint turned slightly in his seat. Maxine Van Alen had burst through the doors, looking frazzled. He didn't see her clients.

"I'm sorry we're late, Judge," she said. "My clients just arrived."

But they clearly hadn't caught up yet. Flint glanced at the front of the courtroom. Luc Deshin looked flustered. Celestine Gonzalez, who had once helped Flint with some legalities concerning Talia, had folded her hands in front of her stomach.

Deshin's wife had turned slightly in her seat, and so did her frightened young son.

"We plan to fight this adoption, your honor," Van Alen said as she walked to the front of the courtroom. "We were sandbagged here, with no time to prepare—"

"On the contrary, Ms. Van Alen," the judge said. "You had years to prepare for this. I'm not even sure your clients have standing."

"They do, your honor," she said. "They're the biological parents."

"Who Disappeared," the judge said.

"The charges against them have been dropped," Van Alen said. "They have returned, ready to resume their lives."

"Six and a half years later," the judge said. "An eternity in the life of a child."

The little boy straightened. Flint frowned. The child knew they were talking about him. Flint wasn't even sure the boy should be here, but it wasn't Flint's call.

Flint's companion hadn't shown up yet either. He had told Selah Rutledge to come to the courthouse. He had told her the Grazians would be here.

If she was smart, she would bring the police officers who had handled this morning's attack with her. He had told her to do so, but she had harrumphed him, like she often did. He could never tell if that meant she agreed with him or disagreed with him.

Footsteps echoed outside the door. He turned again, expecting to see Selah.

Instead, two people he had only seen in surveillance imagery walked through. A husband and wife, looking washed out and frightened, wearing the same clothes they had worn that morning.

The Grazians.

And as they entered, they looked at no one except the little boy, shivering up front.

24

It was them. His mom hadn't told him they would be here. Paavo grabbed her arm so hard that she gasped, but she didn't pull away. Instead, she pulled him closer.

His heart was pounding so hard that it hurt. They were coming closer and closer and closer, and he wanted to bury his face in his mom's neck, but he couldn't. He didn't dare look away from them.

"Are they really here?" he asked his mom.

She nodded.

They were only a meter or so away. The woman reached out for him—

And he couldn't help it. He screamed. He screamed and backed up, nearly falling off the bench. His dad pulled him against the columned fence between the bench and the table, holding him. His mom stood in front of him, blocking his view.

"Stay away!" Paavo screamed. "Stay away!"

"Ms. Gonzalez," the judge said. "Do something to soothe that child."

"Is there somewhere safe he can go?" Paavo's mother asked.

Safe. They wanted him safe. Paavo leaned against his dad. That woman was still staring at him, trying to say something, but he wasn't going to listen. He wouldn't listen.

"My chambers," the judge said.

His mom picked him up. His dad said he could do it, but she said, no, you need to stay here. Then she carried Paavo to the back, through a door that the judge opened for them.

Away from those people. Away.

Until he saw the Ghosts standing in front of him, and he screamed again.

"They're on his links!" his mother screamed. "Make them stop!"

Somehow she knew. She knew.

"If you're interfering with that child," the judge said. "Then—"

The Ghosts disappeared. The door closed. Paavo trembled.

"Are they gone?" his mom asked.

"They're outside," he whispered.

"But you can't see them in here, can you?" she asked.

"No," he said.

"Good." She set him on a soft couch. There was a desk and a window that overlooked the City Center. And a robe hanging from a peg.

"We'll wait in here until they go away," his mom said. "Don't worry, I'll be with you the whole time."

He nodded, as if it made a difference. But she had been with him a lot when he saw the Ghosts, and that usually didn't make them go away. Although that judge lady had helped.

Maybe it would all stop now.

Maybe.

25

"I don't know what you just did," Van Alen said as she helped her clients to the table beside her. "But whatever it was was pretty damn stupid."

Károly Grazian glared at her. Ishani Grazian looked worried. The judge had pulled the door to her chambers closed and resumed her place at the bench.

"These people scare my son, Judge," Luc Deshin said.

His lawyer shushed him.

"That's pretty obvious, Mr. Deshin," the Judge said. "What did you do to that child?"

Van Alen looked at her clients. The question had gone directly to them.

"Nothing," Károly Grazian said.

"That wasn't nothing. That boy is terrified of you and he thought you had gotten into my chambers," the Judge said.

"If I may, Judge," Luc Deshin said. "I know what they did."

His lawyer was shushing him, but it seemed to do no good.

"Quickly, Mr. Deshin."

"They have been using his links since he was a tiny baby. We just found out about it. Grazian here designed links and he messed with Paavo's somehow. Paavo thinks they're Ghosts. He's terrified of them and convinced they'll hurt him."

"They did try to hurt him, Judge," Deshin's lawyer said. "They tried to kidnap Paavo today."

The judge's eyebrows went up.

Van Alen felt her cheeks heat. Flint had been right. She should have left this one alone. She had known nothing about the links.

"Is this true, Counselor?" the judge asked Van Alen.

She turned to her clients. "Is it true?" she asked softly.

Károly stood defiantly, saying nothing.

"Is it true?" Van Alen asked.

"You'll answer or be held in contempt of this court," the judge said.

"We didn't mean to terrorize him," Ishani said. "We just wanted him to remember us. We thought we would be back for him. And we did come back. We're back now."

"Your honor," the lawyer said, "I have submitted all sorts of documentation about the Deshin home. This child is well cared for and loved. Our petition—"

"Is granted," the judge said. "I have no idea why you're even here, Ms. Van Alen. There was nothing to fight. These people abandoned their child six and half years ago. The fact that they've been terrorizing him ever since is just appalling to me."

"It's not terrorizing," Ishani said. "All we did was tell him that we loved him."

The judge looked at Van Alen. "Get them out of my courtroom. *Now.*"

She didn't have to be told twice. She put her hand on their backs and pushed them forward.

"We should fight this," Károly said. "They have no right to take our child."

Van Alen didn't answer him. She didn't dare. She wanted to tell him what an idiot he was, how he had sandbagged his own case, how he was the most insensitive person she had ever represented.

But she didn't, mostly because she wanted them out of her life.

Flint was standing. Van Alen frowned at him. He fell in with them as they went to the door.

"The Deshins took care of your child," Flint said to the Grazians as he walked with them. "They raised him. That was what you wanted, wasn't it?"

Károly looked at him. "Who are you?"

"He was a difficult child," Flint said, "so brilliant and high strung. He cried a lot and he was too much for your wife to handle, wasn't he?"

His questions made Van Alen nervous. She glanced over her shoulder. The judge had opened the door to her chambers, but she was watching.

"What are you doing?" Van Alen whispered to Flint.

"Satisfying my own curiosity," he said.

"He wasn't too much for me to handle," Ishani said. "But Károly worries."

Károly glared at her. Van Alen felt a curious lightness. "What's this all about, Miles?" she asked.

"When it became clear that the baby was too much for Ishani, they wanted someone else to take care of the baby during the difficult early months," Flint said. "But they figured they'd be back when he was old enough to understand reason, and then they'd take him back."

"He should be ours," Ishani said. "I love him."

Not *we*, Van Alen noted. Never *we*.

She pushed open the courtroom doors and stopped. Two police officers in uniform stood there, along with a woman who looked somewhat familiar.

"Almost too late, Selah," Flint said.

The woman smiled at him. The police officers said, "Ishani and Károly Grazian? You're under arrest for attempted kidnapping."

Each officer grabbed a Grazian and pulled their hands behind their backs, securing them with cuffs.

"They can't do this," Ishani said to Van Alen. "He's our son."

"I expect you to come with us," Károly said to Van Alen.

"I'll send my associate," Van Alen said, "until we can find you someone else."

She didn't want anything to do with them. She nodded at her associate, who had been standing just outside the doors. He hurried along with them. He was just six months out of law school. This entire case was over his head, which was just fine with her.

The woman that Flint knew hurried along with them, probably to press her complaint.

"Don't tell me," Van Alen said. "She's the head of the Aristotle Academy."

"That's right," Flint said. He looked at her sideways. "I thought you were going to defend them all the way to the Multicultural Tribunal."

"Sometimes things are much better in theory," Van Alen said.

He smiled at her.

"How did you know they didn't want to raise the child?" she asked.

"A hunch at first," he said. "But I found some evidence. Do you want to see it?"

"No," she said. "I want to be rid of those people. I had forgotten how horrible they were."

"I thought Disappeareds could do no wrong," Flint said.

She made a face at him. "They're human like everyone else."

"But Luc Deshin is a criminal," Flint reminded her.

Van Alen recalled how the little boy had run to his father when he saw the Grazians. His father clearly represented safety to him.

"He's not a criminal to his son," she said.

"Wow," Flint said. "I'm stunned. You backed off of your principles."

"You're not stunned," Van Alen said. "You know I'm not dogmatic."

He smiled at her. "I know."

"But you are," she said.

"Only when it comes to children," he said.

"And your own version of right and wrong," she said.

"That too," he agreed. "That too."

26

It took Paavo a long time to start breathing normally. His dad had come into the room and had his arms wrapped around him. The judge was talking to his parents about legalities and documents and signing things.

Then, she said to Paavo, you'll be theirs.

He already was theirs. She didn't understand that. She hadn't understood a lot of things. He had to explain the Ghosts. She looked upset at that, and she finally ordered someone just outside the door to press some charges against the Ghosts. Something about invasion of privacy and manipulation with the intent to terrorize.

"They'll go away for a long time," she said to Paavo's dad.

"Good," his dad had said.

"And you better straighten up too," she said to Paavo's dad. "Don't think I haven't heard stories."

His dad looked startled. Paavo was. He had never heard anyone talk to his dad like that.

"This boy loves you," the judge said. "You should make sure you're worthy of that love."

Paavo didn't like the way the judge was talking. He glared at her.

"He is worthy," Paavo said. "He's my dad."

ABOUT THE AUTHOR

INTERNATIONAL BESTSELLING WRITER KRISTINE Kathryn Rusch has won or been nominated for every major award in the science fiction field. She has won Hugos for editing *The Magazine of Fantasy & Science Fiction* and for her short fiction. She has also won the *Asimov's Science Fiction Magazine* Readers Choice Award six times, as well as the Anlab Award from *Analog Magazine*, *Science Fiction Age* Readers Choice Award, the Locus Award, and the John W. Campbell Award. Her standalone sf novel, *Alien Influences*, was a finalist for the prestigious Arthur C. Clarke Award. *Io9* said her Retrieval Artist series featured one of the top ten science fiction detectives ever written. She writes a second sf series, the Diving Universe series, as well as a fantasy series called The Fey. She also writes mystery, romance and fantasy novels, occasionally using the pen names Kris DeLake, Kristine Grayson and Kris Nelscott.

The Retrieval Artist Series:

wMG
Publishing

Made in the USA
San Bernardino, CA
11 April 2013